IMMORTAL   *Erik Jayce Landberg*

I0547809

IMMORTAL   *Erik Jayce Landberg*

IMMORTAL

By

ERIK JAYCE LANDBERG

Victoria Publishing Ltd.

ISBN 978-1-105-64425-2

Thanks to Xandra Alkemade.

IMMORTAL   *Erik Jayce Landberg*

IMMORTAL

By

ERIK JAYCE LANDBERG

IMMORTAL   *Erik Jayce Landberg*

IMMORTAL

IMMORTAL   *Erik Jayce Landberg*

IMMORTAL

In a time devoured by the sole and absurd obsession of eternal youth, Mike seizes the microphone not quite in enthusiasm. His shirt is of a dazzling blue, his tie undone just beneath the collar streak. His forehead is ghastly with sweat, yet not so much out of nervousness as of enthusiasm.

Outside autumn leaves are falling to a certain fate as the wind unleashes gusts of air against the frail window blinds of the lecture room. It whistles through as if to remind of the sour demise of a summer that once was but no longer is. It does so only to hush seconds later, entailing that nothing lasts forever. Or does it?

The year is 2047. A year consumed by progress. That of Botox, hair transplant solutions, anti-wrinkle creams, and many other breakthroughs, the essence of which has driven society to the inevitable dependency where growing old, or at least being perceived as such is no longer an option.

It is a year in which promises of eternal youth and the supremacy of words are more highly sought after than the boredom or reality.

"What if I told you," Mike began. He paused briefly, seeking to meet gazes. "…that there is a way you will never grow old? Would you believe me?"

There were half a dozen or so in the crowd whose faces could be recognized from the previous lecture, the week earlier.

"Would you be willing to do whatever it takes to achieve eternal life?

Mike always started his lessons with those very two sentences, as if he wanted to catch the attention of his apprentices all at once.

And they kept coming back, week after week, month after month. His listeners, same faces every time. Several were new of course, and while some were used to the stark, almost rusty voice of his, others were discovering his fervor for the very first time.

They had heard of him of course. How couldn't they when so many notorious scientific newspapers and magazines had covered him at least once over the past three years.

Had it not been for thundering roars thumping across from afar, silence would have dawned on the room and roared across its dark wooden walls. Everyone in it held their breath in attentiveness, as though fully absorbed by the magic of his words.

Yet some remained unconvinced, attending his speeches with narrow-mindedness and prejudice. After all, the press had referred to him as *"the ultimate mad scientist"*, a stamp strong enough to arouse the curiosity of even the most sceptical amongst them, it seemed.

Rain started to beat down on the grey streets about the block as Mike dashed down the concrete steps of the building opening on Grosvenor Street. One of the attendees hastened behind him in a staggering motion as though to avoid the slippery stains.

Casting a swift glance beyond his shoulder, he tried to head her off as he often did with seemingly stalking critics or journalists.

"Mr. Heathrow?" she bellowed as he leaped around the corner heading for the other side of California street.

She stopped short of the zebra crossing, to her chagrin the light faded to red. From afar she could still make out his black soaked umbrella disappearing beyond the park. She might still stand a chance she thought, yet panting for air and craving for the light to turn back to green.

As seconds leaped and cars hummed through, her hand dug into the leather of her worn, black purse seemingly in an endeavor to conceal a device.

Lights turned green.

She cast a quick glance to her right, at the skyscrapers overlooking Chinatown as though to remind herself how to head back to Grosvenor Suite where she temporarily rented a flat. Rain began to pour all the more as she dashed after her prey.

She was now in the park, the French Cathedral on her left. Before her eyes the street began to get steeper all the way down to Fisherman's Wharf. Her ankle was aching and she thought what an ordeal it would be to walk back up again would Mr. Heathrow decide to stroll down the avenue.

In the meantime he was nowhere to be seen. She had paused, panting for air and reaching down again into her leather purse. Her gaze drowned in it as though in chase of a hiding prey.

She dug out the device but dropped it inadvertently as it fell down on the crosswalk with a thud. Raindrops began to stain its silver metallic shelf. She bent forward to pick it up when out of the blue a reddish ray lit up on the upper left. It looked like a screen display yet seemed to be something else.

She held it in her palm, her eyes examining it in awe. A passer-by cast a quick glance in her direction as he strolled past her. For a very brief moment she'd swear there was suspicion in his gaze. She didn't linger and tossed the device back into her purse when all of a sudden footsteps emerged. In a twinkle of an eye she had turned around to face the man behind her.

She opened her mouth.

"I… I'm not a–"

"I know you're not a journalist" the man answered still concealing his face beneath his umbrella.

"I followed you to–"

"I know why you followed me," he interrupted, his face still in the shadows.

"How do you mean?" Her voice quivered a bit.

"The device."

"You forgot it in the auditorium… I just wanted to return it to you," she smiled in nervousness.

"I left it there on purpose to attract you here," he answered now revealing his traits.

"You left it on my table on your way out, Mr. Heathrow and…" She paused. "To lead me here…?"

"Precisely."

"I… I don't understand," she stammered in her sweet British accent.

He didn't answer.

"What is this all about Mr. Heathrow?" she sighed as her gaze tensely ran down and stroked her feet.

"Call me Mike."

"What is this all about, Mike? What exactly is it that you want?"

"You want to know what that device is and I want to know–"

"What makes you think I want to know anything Mr. Heathrow?" she rose her voice as though gaining confidence.

"Look let's stop pretending for a minute, " he smirked in wryness. "You've been attending each and every one of my lectures, sitting in the exact same place every time, hearing me rehash the same old speech over and over again, each time for new students, each time for different faces save for yours. Your face was always there, identical, perpetual," he paused, "obsolete."

"So…?" she smiled and waved her head. There is a couple of dozen who keep coming back to your speeches."

"They're journalists."

"I ain't–"

"I know you're not. See I couldn't help but notice your beautiful gaze and all the questions sparkling in it, dissecting with greed my gear from head to toe, longing for answers, dying for answers."

"What do you want to know?" she sighed as she shrugged.

Rain kept beating down on Mike's umbrella.

"I know you're not a journalist, nor an avid student. I'll tell you all you want to know if you tell me who you are and who you work for."

"Very well…"

"Over a coffee."

***

From the outside the Diner appeared forsaken. A few oaks swayed in the wind as though to attest the place was not entirely desolate. Although the rain had set at last, a muggy mist still prevailed outside as though to confine people in. Reminiscent of the tempest was the hush of the wind stroking the blinds and the wet sound of tyres of a few cars driving by on the other side of the green firs by the parking lot.

Inside a smoky atmosphere stanched and blurred the windows overlooking Union Square.

"Milk, sir?"

Mike answered the waitress with a slight nod for all to judge, yet absorbed by the discussion.

"I'm going to be totally honest with you," he pursued as he stirred the coffee. "I think I know exactly who your employer is, I just want it confirmed and hear it from your own mouth before we take this discussion any further."

She pulled a wry smile as her eyes were drawn to her cup.

"I would very much doubt so, Mr. Heathrow."

"Try me. What do you know about SIT?"

She raised her eyebrows.

"Not much except it's very classified from what I understand and that…"

"Yes?"

"Well there are a lot of rumors surrounding it."

"So I would believe," he uttered as he took a sip.

Silence dawned briefly on the moment until she dared to ask.

"What is it?"

"Does the term E.O.P.A. ring a bell?"

"No," she replied as though she was asking a question.

"Let's cut the crap here will you? I know exactly what your deeds are. They sent you on a mission to find out haven't they?

"Who?"

"The European Opposition Project against America, you know damn well what I'm talking about!"

Her eyebrows betrayed her once more. So did her gaze as she looked down again with panting breath.

"What would their interest possibly be in your program?"

"You tell me. What does the word Opposition entail?"

"Mr. Heathrow." She rose abruptly from her chair and grabbed her purse. "I think I'd better take my leave now, if you would excuse–"

"What if I told you I'm intending to divulge everything to you right here right now in this coffee shop."

"I don't think so…"

She turned around and began strolling towards the exit.

"Miss Crowney, you're forgetting something," he uttered out loud with such self confidence that she paused almost before he had finished saying her name. "My device's still in your purse."

Slowly, she turned around so as to face him.

"How do you know my na–?"

"Are you in or out?"

He took yet another sip, his eyes still avoiding hers.

"What's the catch?"

"You get to work for me. You tell them everything I tell you to. Whatever they pay you I'll double it."

"A twofold spy, huh?"

***

The next day bore the scars of the tempest. It rose above a rusty Golden Gate, the color of which was barely reminiscent of red. "Why did they ever stop to paint this bridge?" he mumbled to himself as he drove under the climbing towers soaring past above his head.

2023 was the year it all started. The ever-growing unemployment rate, the deficient economy leaving Europe and most countries outside the United States on the brink. 2023 also saw the fall of the European economy, the abandon of the Euro currency and the excommunication of several latin countries from the E.U. Wasn't it all inevitable after the big crash of 2017. At least it helped the United States re-assert its position as a world leading economy after the Bush Government. Yet the country was still unstable and its overgrowing population and crime rate didn't make it much easier. Did it?

As if that wasn't enough, dazzling conspiracy rumors about viruses implemented by the U.S. government with the aim of cutting down the population began to spread like the plague.

One thing led to another. Suspicion aroused obsession and before the end of the 30's the masses became infatuated with the notion of eternal youth and the postponing of death. All that contributed of course to Mike Heathrow's ingenious idea. An idea so ingenious that he had acquired a greater amount of enemies than friends over the past three years.

Among the foes, a specific group of readers of course; the ever-growing lefty E.O.P.A. who had, in this turbulent political and cultural climate, gained increasing respect here in the U.S. It is an anti-American movement counteracting newly born American values which they judge far too plastic and superficial and which they refer to as a national threat to European traditions.

And who could work as a darker menace than Mr. Mike Heathrow himself?

Long had their eyes dissected his manuscripts. Long had their ears lurked in dark corners and attended his lectures. Long had their minds apprehended the fact that his ideas were grandiose if not revolutionary.

Long had they realized that his scientific assets were jeopardizing their frail ideologies.

He parked the car on the steep road leading up to California Street. Nob Hill wasn't what it used to be anymore, he thought as he turned off the engine and threw a sideways glance in the rear-view mirror. If everything goes according to plan he pictured, this street, let alone the neighborhood would become a very different place. A smirk formed at the corner of his mouth as he locked the door behind him. This time he would use the back door he thought so as to avoid tabloid journalists and the scandal press. After all he had only invited what he perceived to be the real press. The big wheel as he often referred to it.

Mason Hotel glowed white in the morning sun. The conference room shrieked with inquisitiveness under the entering steps of a thousand or so curious lads invited to hear very special words (they were told).

She grabbed a different seat and this time her gaze was no longer drawn to the mysterious device of his. For she knew didn't she? She knew it all and he was going to use her as a diversion. As a means to not arouse suspicion or doubts as regards to the STI project, which he knew they would never let happen, if it came to their knowledge.

"What if I told you?" he began.

Before his eyes, hordes of bloodthirsty paparazzi glared as he spoke the next controversial words.

"That I have created a brand new world in which you all can live forever…"

Eyebrows frowned.

Faces lit up.

Smirks vanished.

"…and where death is obsolete?"

***

The door slammed as her high heels echoed on the marble floor of Lorry's Diner. The penetrating sun through the blinds cast her silhouette in a blend of shades and smoke.

At the rear Mike lifted his cup and brought it shy of his lips. He blew twice with an outstanding calm.

"Why did you divulge everything?" the silhouette questioned loudly.

There was anger in her voice and her lips shivered as she uttered the next words.

"I just can't believe you did it! How are you supposed to get the project approved by the White House? It is the most foolish–"

"Take a seat, Vanessa!" he countered flatly as he took a sip.

"Mr Heathrow!" she raised her voice.

"Please."

He waved at her, aiming at the seat in front of him, yet without the respect of meeting her gaze.

There was self-assurance and an ounce of arrogance in the way he waved.

Astonishing was the fact that she complied without much resistance.

Her tone smoothed when she continued;

"There where a hundred paparazzi or so there, some from major magazines and press institutions."

"The big wheel," he smirked.

"What would make you do something like that? You're digging your own grave."

"Because there is another spy from the E.O.P.A.! You don't seriously believe that they would rely entirely on your accounts?"

His gaze met with hers but only shortly.

"What?"

"I was forced to divulge part of it in order to dissolve any suspicion or distrust that they may hold towards me."

"I don't understand," she sighed as her eyes fell down to the table and she shook her head.

Instead of lying totally about the SIT project which they wouldn't buy, I chose to undermine it by means of you." He leaned forward towards her. "You see, you are gonna tell them there is no threat." His tone worsened. "You are gonna tell them my project is merely the work of a madman, a utopia that doesn't stand a chance and whose credibility is ridiculous. That this whole thing isn't feasible and that there is no more to it than an ordinary virtual experience, void of any consequences for humanity. To make a long story short, you will tell them my program doesn't work and that I'm only thirsting for fame scoops and financial gratification."

"Why me?"

"Because you're not like them."

She stroked her purse as though thinking it all over.

"Vanessa." He said her name as though he had known her for years. "All I want is to buy enough time for it to reach the White House. They are everywhere, among senators, lawyers, mothers, daughters. Like cockroaches. Would they only lay eyes on as little as the project's synopsis, the whole project would be over. Like this!"

He snapped his fingers.

She frowned at the sound as though scared or intimidated by it.

"Do you understand me? This is my only chance to get it through."

Had there been the slightest arrogance in his voice just a moment before, it was now as far as last winter's snow.

She shook her head only to stammer.

"I... I don't know," she whispered flatly.

"You're not gonna let the American conspiracy carry out this bloodless genocide are you?" he exclaimed with a deep sigh.

She kept her head down and brought her hands to her face. She sank it in her palms.

"God knows there is not enough place on this planet. Soon people will die everyday. The economy is dead. There will not be enough food to feed everyone. The threat is imminent. It's all over the place. An impending doom! They're creating this mass psychosis and obsession about eternal youth to create a diversion in people's minds so that no one sees what's going on under the mantel."

She raised her eyes and her gaze confronted his for the first time in several minutes.

"Don't you understand, Vanessa?" he pursued. "I'm offering the world an exit, a solution to everything where there will never be too little space. Where an overpopulated world is obsolete and where resources are infinite."

"You're also creating a problem," she countered with firmness in her voice.

He paused, leaned back on his seat, then leaned forward again.

"What do you mean?"

"You are creating a major problem for the establishment. They'll never let you go through with this. You'll jeopardize your life and the lives of others! Including mine."

"Oh so that's what puzzles you? You're frightened and more concerned 'bout your safety than the fight for a good cause?"

No sooner had he said the words than she pointed her finger at him.

"Don't even try, Mr. Heathrow!"

"I know it's not the case, Miss Vanessa Crowney. And therefore you have no excuse but to get involved in this," he smiled.

She returned the smile, nervously.

***

"What do you mean by '*program*', Mr Heathrow?"
"It's a virtual world where no mistakes can be made."

"A virtual world?" the former voice counter-asked.

"You can lower your hand, sir." He waved flatly making that hand-raised silhouette appear as though he was no more important to him than a little tabloid paper thriving to get *in* the game. Little did the others know he represented a major paper.

"Yes a virtual world."

"Critics have claimed the program doesn't work," another voice in the crowd uttered.

"How so?" Mike seized the water and took a sip without raising so much as an eyebrow, calm as an eye in a storm.

"Even *Post-modern Science Magazine* said it won't work because it lacks one essential motor, namely a device capable of refraining the program from rebooting and thus refrain all stored information from being lost would a general power failure occur."

"A power failure?" Mike coughed a bit as he jested in amusement. He put the little plastic bottle back by the microphone stand.

"I'm not talking about a standard power failure Mr. Heathrow, I'm talking about a general power seizure in which the continuity of the virtual time continuum would be altered and cease to exist."

"Here you go…" he shrugged. "Have you ever heard of the term Girophony, Mr…?" He paused as though genuinely interested in his name.

"No," the voice uttered flatly.

"It is a device imagined by an inventor about a little more than half a century ago."

"And?" another voice shouted from the far rear of the conference room.

"And…" Mike tucked a gum into his mouth. "…I suggest you do some research and put some thought into it. It's a device whose essential feature is to relocate, or redirect if you will, sound signals, as the source of the sound generically moves onward. In this case a similar engineering directly borrowed from the Girophony, redirects energy sources as the virtual time continuum proceeds forward. Thus any power failure would already be in the past when the failure occurs and becomes therefore obsolete. *O.B.S.O.L.E.T.E,* Mr. whoever you are."

He spelled the word with such sarcasm that silence dawned on the crowd. Whether it was in convincement or bewilderment before the arrogance of the man would be hard to ascertain but his egotism surely convinced some of them yet only caused a wry smirk to form in the corner of Vanessa's mouth.

***

The plane took off more abruptly than it landed. Vanessa had stared at the clouds passing by, finding it hard to believe that under this radiant sunshine, soaring above these clouds, mist and snow awaited below.

It was no little delusion when they finally vanished and gave way to a view of skyscrapers screaming above a realm of haze.

"Why did you bring up the Girophony?" she asked as they both stepped into the yellow cab.

"Because it's clear that it doesn't work." He lit a cigarette.

"So he was right?"

Mike threw a quick glance at the driver in front of him.

"Mind if I smoke?"

The driver answered by shrugging and waved his hand in the rear-view mirror as if to say *You already lit it didn't you?*

"Of course he was right," he exhaled as he took a deep drag on the filter. *More* had always been his favorite brand and he'd make sure those long brown cigarillo-look alike death sticks linger on in what he now referred to as *the new world* and occasionally as *the brand new world* to avoid Orwell's term *brave*.

"So what was the point in lying?" she asked in astonishment.

"You almost disappoint me, Vanessa."

"How so?" she retorted.

The cab driver's gaze stroked the rear-view mirror.

"You probably noticed the overconfidence of my tone during my speech," he lowered his voice almost to a whisper.

She answered with a nod.

"If I can convince them that I'm so self-absorbed as to believe a half decade old device can serve model to a whole computerized virtual reality, the only logical outcome would be for them not to take me seriously and therefore   leave me be. They'll make one or two research attempts to verify the potential and efficiency of the device until they give up on me with a grin."

He grinned himself.

The driver glanced in the rear-view mirror with a staggering gaze.

Vanessa noticed and lowered her voice.

"So you're out to dissuade them from even bothering trying to refrain you," she whispered as though she was sharing a schoolgirl secret.

"We're on the right path. First I throw this meeting in the Big Apple and next stage's Washington. We sneak closer in to the target smooth and easy. It'll all go unnoticed to them."

"What makes you think you'll even get close to the White House?"

"I'll be throwing a few other meetings during the next few weeks in order to confuse them. We'll let the media do their work. In the meantime, as we get closer to Washington I'll start to reveal more and more about the true nature of the program which will catch the attention of essential, targeted politicians, while it'll dissuade the interest of the media and that of the E.O.P.A. and its administration. I'll start right here in New York."

"Targeted politicians?" she frowned.

He lowered his eyes but the driver didn't.

"Mr. Heathrow?" she paused. "Mike?"

Michael leaned toward her.

"Ever heard of Jason Patterson?"

No sooner had he mentioned the name than she raised her eyebrows almost instantly, seemingly in shock.

"Oh so that's what you had in mind! You were just out to use me all along weren't you?" she retorted waving at the driver and summoning him to stop the cab.

Mike grabbed her arm firmly in an attempt to still her down. His lips stroked her ear. His teeth showed as he murmured.

"Regain composure. I'm pleading you."

"Don't even think about it, Mister! I ain't gonna let you use my entourage to achieve your ends!"

She waved again, aiming at the rear-view mirror.

"Senator Patterson is one of your close relatives. He's my only chance to get the project to the Majestic 12 board and eventually to the president!"

His didn't raise his voice but his teeth showed again.

"What do I care! Stop the cab!" she uttered out loud, digging in her purse as though she was looking for keys.

"You know damn well what will happen if we let them go through with their plans! They have a program…" he stammered for the name as it escaped him, "Elite 11, in which they will let everyone die, save for the elite. They will choose eleven people from each race. They will be sheltered and kept in safety for future generations… There won't be any space left… there…"

He lost his words.

She picked up her cell phone and dropped it in inadvertence.

"Please don't leave this cab! I'll explain he's with–" he whispered but she was already shouting back.

"I ain't going nowhere! You're the one who's leaving the cab, Mister!"

"Vanessa… he's–"

"Get OUT!" she spat, emphasizing *out* with such conviction that Mike's renowned conference speeches would have passed for less than a teenager's school resume in front of the class in comparison.

"He's with them," he said out loud as the door slammed before his eyes and the engine roared with screeching tyres down Madison Boulevard.

A horn echoed from afar, leaving him stranded at the corner of Powell's and Fifth.

He turned around.
"Taxi!" he yelled.

***

The next lecture bore the scars of the day in that it was nothing like the former press conferences he had been throwing in California. Vanessa's seat was now empty and as he spoke, Mike seemed elsewhere, his forehead ghastly with sweat and a former self-assurance sadly substituted for a lack of wordiness.

In truth he could think of nothing else but her, and as the questions dashed from the audience like wry, stinging needles his mind was set on his cell phone, perpetually dissecting the screen after a text or a life sign.

"What exactly is the essence of this virtual world Mr. Heathrow?" one needle stung.

He tucked the phone back into the sheltering silk of his suit.

"It is a virtual world, very identical to ours save for one tiny little detail."

He stroked the shell of his costume as though to assure himself the phone was still there. *Just in case* he thought. *Just in case.*

"The magazines talk about a brand new world deprived of imperfection. Imperfection? What's that entail?"

"It means no diseases, no earthquakes, no disasters, no..." he paused, to all appearances agitated and unfocused. "To sum up, it means no negative things whatsoever. Next question please."

He pointed a finger toward a risen hand at the rear of the conference room.

"Is there any better word than *utopia* to qualify your program?"

Laughter burst out, instilling eeriness akin to that of a political debate leading nowhere.

"How would that be?"

"I mean come on!" He looked about as though to get the support of everybody else in the audience. "A perfect world without any negativity? How would that work?"

He shrugged with a smirk.

"I have created a program that is so close to perfection that it provides with the possibility to transfer all information stored in a human brain to the new virtual world in question."

"You mean memories?"

"Memories, data, your entire life as if it had never ceased."

"What do you mean by *ceased*?" a voice uttered from the rear.

"Why would anybody want to have their memories transferred?" another one questioned.

Mike seized his cell again, placing it back on the stand in a flat yet determined gesture, as though to adjourn the *meeting*.

"The good thing," he seemed to regain confidence, "is that neither the transfer nor the program requires the body to function in order for it to work. Hence," he paused.

Had they roared with laughter just a minute ago, they were now sitting in absolute stillness, mouths agape, staring glares, as if they already knew of the words he was about to utter next.

"Hence," he pursued. "The consciousness of the transferred mind will live on forever after the body ceases to exist."

He said the words with such calm and banality that it would have had a paraplegic fall from his chair – had there been paraplegics in the new world to come, that is.

Tumult and moans filled the room as his phrase dawned on them like a thunderclap.

He had clearly said too much. Perhaps even gone too far in his phrasing this time. Yet he stood now at the point of no return. A point where divulging the rest would seem to have no further impact as to the consequences he had unleashed upon himself. Blame it upon his inability to see clear that very day or the simple fact that the secret was too much of a burden to bare.

"Do you realize what you're saying?" a voice uttered from afar.

Somehow he had divulged too much to stop right there.

"In doing so they acquire a new virtual body, a perfect, young one, not the least subjected to diseases or mortality. "Is that what you meant by living forever, Dr. Heathrow?"

Mike let the question pass unnoticed. Instead, he went ahead, dissecting every corner of the program and its infinite advantages for human kind.

Now that Vanessa was no longer here, he thought as he glanced at his cell phone, there would be no use for her. Nor would it be necessary to conceal certain aspects as he had planned prior to her leaving. Might as well lay all the cards on the table.

"Even so, the newly acquired body will retain past memories and its former consciousness. Thus, in the eyes of the subject, it will merely appear like a faint transfer from the previous real world and the physical body. Some will not even notice a transformation took place. Such is the truthfulness of the new world. It is by its appearance so close to ours that it will basically go unnoticed.

"You keep pointing out the pros. But what are the cons of such a project, Dr. Heathrow?"

"Well, you tell me folks! In a world devoid of famine, natural disasters, poorness, wars, and I skip many. What can the cons possibly be?"

"There must be a catch!" a voice retorted from the first row.

"What about food supplies, and space?" another one asked.

"I return you the question, sir. What about food supplies and the growing lack of space here on Earth? How will you solve that ordeal in the physical world where such resources are physically limited?"

Silence dawned.

"Well?" he smiled, his confidence resurfacing.

Aside from the sound of one or two coughing among them, there was no answer.

"The advantages that I have provided only constitute the tip of the iceberg. Allow me to enlighten you as regards to the matter. The program is generated and maintained by a giant computer here in the physical world. But that's the one and only physical aspect to it. In other words, everybody–"

"Everybody gets a nice, big house and as much money and food as he wants to eat?" a voice interrupted.

Mike grinned.

"Something like that. Although I would have chosen more eloquent words to describe it."

"How can that be?"

"Yes how can all negative events and disadvantages be erased like that? It's a utopia!"

"I told you. Everything is computer generated in the physical world. Basically, to make a long story short, there are two computers working hand in hand. One of them is provided with an infinite hard drive storing all imaginable negativity. Hence, events such as earthquakes, deaths, disasters etc. have been programmed one by one in that very computer. It acts as a counterbalance to all positive equations stored in the second computer. And by no means have we omitted one single negative equation. They're all there, you name it!"

Before their astounded expressions, Mike realized he had created a perfect world for which there would now be nothing but a frantic mass hysteria.

Unsolicited, a voice spoke from nowhere;

"How is Miss Crowney involved in your plans?"

At the words, Mike peered out at the audience.

"Who said that?" he bellowed as he scrutinized every face he was able to see.

But there were many.

"What about the financial side of it? Have you found invest–"

"Who asked that?" Mike retorted but as voices mounted under unquenchable curiosity, question started to build up upon question, and before he could even try to discern his subject, he was soon overwhelmed with an uncontrollable chaos of snapshot flashes and jostling.

Without lingering, he profited from the tumult to make himself scarce, springing straight for the back-door.

In a twinkle of an eye he was out, bolting on Twenty-Third toward his Chevrolet. It was parked down the junction. He ran through the park, heading for Madison, and just as he was about to insert the key, his cell began to ring.

He cast a quick glance at the screen which read *unknown number*, then entered the car so as to answer.

No sooner had he put the phone against his ear than a tarnished voice spoke.

"I believe you are looking for me?"

In the background, Mike could hear traffic and sirens, only to draw a quick link with the street noise about him. At the other end of the line, he heard an ambulance. Then seconds later he heard and saw it drive past him on East Twenty-Third.

"Where are you?" were the only words that came to his mind.

"In the park," the voice replied flatly as the ambulance veered toward Flatiron.

With stapled breath, Mike threw the door open and jumped out of his car. He peered out at the trees, the benches, the people but to no avail.

"You won't find me," the voice continued. "I'm well hidden. But I can see you."

"Who are you? What do you want?"

The voice spoke with such flatness that it made the hair on Mike's arm stand on end.

"Let's put it this way," the voice puffed, as though it was smoking a cigarette, "You have something I care for, and… I would like to think that I have something you care for too."

Mike scrutinized every inch of the park, approaching slowly as he listened. From afar he saw someone take a drag on a cigarette but, as he looked more attentively, it turned out to be a woman.

"I don't know what you're talking about."

He peered all the more.

"Oh come on, Mikey! You didn't think you'd impress us with that silly, little speech of yours? Girophony? Who the fuck are you kidding?"

"I still don't k–"

"We know the program works. We know your intentions and we're not gonna let you go through with it."

In the background, Mike could still hear the same street noise that surrounded him.

"You can't stop me!"

"Once we get the code, we'll just change it so that you can't initiate it."

"The program's activation code is sealed. You'll never get it."

"Is that so?"

Mike could almost hear the voice at the other end grin.

His heavy Southern accent was too much to bare for him and, as he swore he saw someone with a cell, obscured by a tree, the obscure voice uttered in threat;

"Does the name Crowney ring a bell? Or perhaps it spells *Clown*ey?"

Mike pretended as though he hadn't uncovered him and took his time to answer so as to win time and sneak in closer.

"Are you blackmailing me?" he uttered after a brief pause.

"Smart guy for a scientist, Heathrow."

"If you hurt her I'll make sure to–"

"To what? You'll make sure not to include me in your delusional, virtual, brand new world?"

"How do we proceed?"

"You mail the code to *13@codex.com* along with the exact I.P. of the server powering the computer generator. Once we verify it and erase the entire hard drive, we'll release her and she'll be safe and sound. It's as simple as that."

"How can I trust you will?"

"I give you five hours. Beyond that she dies."

The voice hung up on him with a disturbing tick, and just as he did, Mike saw his subject let go of his phone and throw it in a wastebasket behind the trees.

On a whim, he began dashing toward him as fast as he could, praying he wouldn't turn around, praying he could catch his prey unawares. But to his dismay, the man in the black coat did, and as their eyes met, only a few yards apart, the same man pulled out a firearm shooting twice at him. Mike dove forward and crashed aside in a commotion of screams and shouts from passer-bys. and as he lifted his eyes from the concrete surrounding him, the man had vanished, leaving no clue behind but the cell in the trash.

Mike jumped to his feet and sprang for the basket with stapled breath. He reached with both hands and began digging as though he had been a bum starving his guts out. He ploughed and ploughed, but to his deception, the cell was nowhere to be found.

He turned around and saw a man tuck something in his shirt.

"Hey you over there!" he shouted but the man didn't so much as give him a sideways glance.

Instead the pace of his steps increased as he walked away from him, back toward East Twenty-Third. Mike did his best to follow, but his left leg hurt too much after his fall on the concrete. Hence, plucking up his courage, he staggered back to the Chevrolet thinking how lucky he was that the gunman missed him by a fraction. He sank into the front seat painstakingly and reached for the glove compartment. His hands were shaking but eventually he managed to dig out the mysterious device of his. He held it firmly in his palm and scrolled down along the silver-blue screen. Before his eyes, mysterious numbers passed, unheard of. It looked as if they were some kind of language or cryptogram that needed to be deciphered.

Mike pondered. Could he really give them the code? He had worked so hard for this to happen, he frowned. As much as the thought weighed on him, *what's one life sacrificed in order to save billions?* and even though science had taught him never to mix feelings with the tasks, that thought repulsed him irrefutably. *It was out of the question – come what may – but it was out of the question.*

– Period –

He raised his eyes to examine the street, as though in search of a clue, when all of a sudden, it dawned on him like a thousand bricks from above. Vanessa had dropped her cell. Had she not? Just before she left him stranded, there in the middle of nowhere, yet in the middle of New York. He recalled how she threw him out of the yellow cab and how he had wanted to tell her. But there was no time. For what he really wanted to tell her about, was the man, the driver in the rear-view mirror.

No holds barred, he inserted the key and turned the engine on. It roared heatedly as he embarked on Madison. Reversed gear in, he backed for East Twenty-Third under the screech of tyres and blowing horns, and no sooner had he braked than the tyres screamed again as he hit the gas toward the street his assailant had disappeared down.

With one hand on the steering wheel, he started dialling a number on his cell, then put it to his ear. He missed a Pontiac by only an inch or so, in an attempt to pass a truck expelling thick plumes of sooty diesel exhaust. Horns blew behind him as he roared past the junction and the red lights.

"Ronald? Ronald? Do you hear me? – Yes – I don't have time to explain – Yes – I need you to track her cell for me. Can you do that? – Two, One, Two – Five, Seven, Seven…"

He enumerated the numbers in a tense, yet confident voice.

"As I said – Yes – I don't have time to explain. They gave me less than five hours. Yeah – I'll be eternally grateful, man!"

As his Chevrolet dashed down the last junction of the avenue, the wait he was forced to undergo felt like an endless ordeal.

"Garment District? Yeah – I got that – Heading toward West Twenty-Third? That's only a few blocks away!"

"Mike, I have located your position too! The vehicle in which the cell is trapped is veering to the right now. You won't cross him but–"

"Tell me the street!"

"Alright, alright, I got it, Roland spoke in his heavy New Yorker accent. "The vehicle seems to have stopped exactly at 563 West 38ᵗʰ Street!"

"Thanks, *pal*!" he retorted as though he had been American himself, but the British intonation ruined the attempt.

In the fourteen years or so that Mike had know Ronald, he had never walked out on him. Not once. Not ever, since they met and worked on the M.C.Y.I.T. project development in Houston back in 2025.

Once at 10ᵗʰ avenue, Mike braked hastily and veered to the right where he began to slowly reverse down 38ᵗʰ. He drove past a few rundown buildings until he finally parked the car, just short of a large parking lot on the right. In the distance, rising above the skyline, two silver-blue skyscrapers reminiscent of the Twins before they collapsed forty-six years ago, soared with majestic pride, but they were too small to even compare, he thought as he slowly but surely snuck out of the car.

"This place hasn't been taken care of since the year 2000," he mumbled as his gaze wandered in search of a clue. The dire reflection of the towers blinded him, and just as his eyes were drawn to a yellow cab parked at the far end of the lot, in the corner, a mysterious pick-up truck swerved in and stopped right behind it.

Mike kneeled down, sheltered by an old rusty Mercedes, the tyres of which were rotten to the core. He observed as two men wearing black shades stepped out and sprang around the corner of the rundown building to the right. They wore dark silk suits and their shoes reflected beams of sunlight as they walked past the shabby two-floor hangar next to the lot. Above the entrance, a faded inscription read *537*. Mike understood at once who the men were, for the number above the door was a secret code used by the E.O.P.A. at the dawn of their arising, before infiltrating into every European establishment.

No sooner had they vanished into the building than Mike started bolting for the cab. He stopped shy of its door, panting for air. The heat surrounding him had become unbearable he thought, as he peered inside the back window. He tried to open the door but the handle wouldn't give. Moreover, the reflection of the sun made it difficult for him to discern anything inside.

He grimaced. Sweat was running down his temples and his mouth felt dry. He gazed to the left. The white pick-up truck caught his attention once again, as if to lure him in. He crawled toward it. The keys were still inside, hanging under the wheel as though to lure him even more.

"They will be back anytime," he managed to sigh as he plucked up the courage and pulled down the handle. The door gave in with a slight creek. In the glove compartment, there were two Nine Millimetres and some gadgets that looked like F.B.I. devices. Without lingering, he seized one of the guns and headed back for the cab.

The back window cracked almost at once, as he battered it with the weapon, and there, lying on the floor, screaming to be noticed; Vanessa's cellular phone.

"They won't be long," he thought as he placed the phone in the pick-up's glove compartment and closed the door so as to steer clear of any suspicion.

Under cover of an abandoned bus, he waited for the men to return, yet to no avail it seemed. Minutes passed and almost turned into what felt as a whole hour. The heat began to take its toll and eventually, Mike saw no other alternatives but to go for it. He found a silver ladder at the back of the building and began climbing with vigilance past the first floor which was plunged in shadows. Mike was able to look closely; nothing but a builder's yard inside. The second floor had now become the target, and as he drew near the windowpane he heard voices inside.

At first, he thought he perceived two male voices, one of which was the man he had spoken to on the phone back at Madison, by the park. But as discussions progressed he heard a third one. It sounded faint and pale, and aside from the fact that it wasn't a male's voice, Mike didn't recognized it straight away. It was not until one of the men asked her to shut her mouth that it dawned on him. It was that of Vanessa. Poor, weak Vanessa whom, judging from the timbre in her throat, had been mistreated badly.

Mike hoped for the best, yet deep inside he knew it would take more than a miracle to get her out of there alive. As a scientist, he had never been much of a believer in God, yet at that very instant, and perhaps for the first time in his entire life, he could swear he heard a quiet prayer pass through his mind. Almost unwittingly.

He frowned and peered inside cautiously, his eyes barely above the pane. There were two silhouettes. One to all appearances holding a gun, the other one, a cell phone. In the center of the room, tied up to a chair, head bowed down; another shadow. That of Vanessa.

They were a few yards away and their backs were turned against him. That gave him a chance to lift the window without being heard and sneak in unnoticed. He ran for cover behind a dusty shelf, almost relieved from the heat. He strove to breathe as little as he could and lent ears.

"Three and a half hours to go," one of them emphasized as he glanced at his watch.

Probably a Rolex, Mike thought as its reflection beamed before his eyes.

"He will never give you the code," Vanessa uttered in a faint, exhausted voice.

The other man walked up to her chair and slapped her forcefully.

"That's it! No more water for you, Ma'am!" he retorted before drawing a cigarette from inside his suit.

He lit it by way of a silver lighter which reflected Vanessa's disillusioned gaze.

"Of course he will, Mr. Glenn–," the other man replied almost shyly.

"How many times did I tell you never to call me by my name, you illiterate idiot?"

"Sorry–"

"You might as well go back to being a taxi driver, Hank! I ain't paying you to behave in such an unprofessional way!"

Mike did his best to remain quiet and pass unnoticed, but as the discussion took a more severe turn, he scarcely lost his temper.

"You're not really going to kill her, Mr. Glennhard? Now are you?

He pulled a deep drag on his cigarette and answered with a grin. "It all depends on Heathrow. It's all in his hands."

Vanessa grunted and coughed as he blew the smoke in her face, antagonizing Mike's wrath even more.

"But now that you mentioned my name in front of her, I have no choice, now do I?"

His grin didn't vanish.

He leaned above her again and just as he prepared to slap her one more time, Mike reflexively hit the edge of the shelf with his elbow, causing a carton box to dive to the floor.

"There's someone in here! Quick, pull out your gun!"

As their gaze wandered within four walls, wiping the whole hangar to and fro, Glennhard pressed the canon of his revolver against Vanessas's left temple.

"I suggest you reveal yourself before I put a bullet in her beautiful skull, Heathrow!"

"Then I might as well not give you the code!" Mike retorted, as he remained hidden in the shadows.

His voice echoed against the walls, which made it impossible for the two men to locate him.

"This is no joke, Heathrow! I'm counting to nine. You're not out by nine and I shoot her! Understand?"

"If you shoot her, you're shooting every chance to lay your hands on the code!" Mike shouted back from behind the dusty shelf.

"One, two—"

"You just don't get it do you? The code is inside of her. It was implemented in her system on a digital crystal screen!"

"Four, five—"

"The code is engraved on the crystal, you need a microscope to retrieve it," Mike bellowed again, but his words didn't seem to affect Glennhard in the least.

"Six–"

"Perhaps he's right, Mr. Glenn–"

"Seven… No he's not! He's only bluffing you fool! Eight!"

"What if he's not bluffing? You know how much's at stake."

Glennhard stopped counting. His eyes were glaring fiercely. He was biting his lips. The taxi driver stared back at him in apprehension.

"Are you ready to come out now, Heathrow? I'll give you the benefit of the doubt!"

Mike didn't make as much as a sound.

Glennhard waited, short of breath.

"Heathrow?"

The two men gave each other one last look.

"Very well, Mikey. I'll shoot her then!"

He lifted the gun towards her, released the magazine only to insert it back in with a loud click, and just as he was about the to pull the trigger, Mike stepped out of the shadows, both of his hands tucked into his pockets, as though utterly unaffected.

"Don't shoot, Glennhard. I'll give you the code."

The gun was still pointing at her right temple. Glenngard's eyes glared as he gazed back at him.

"But I want you to release her first."

"I thought the code was inside her," he answered in sarcasm.

"Bull, as you figured it out yourself. The code is with me. Right here, right now."

Glennhard stared back without a word, his gun still glimmering at arm's length. He gave the driver a slight nod as a command to untie her.

"Put your hands in the air!" he ordered as Vanessa was pulled up to her feet, sobbing. "Now the code, Mr. Heathrow?"

He dug out a crystal sheet no thicker than a credit card and held it up so that they could see it clearly.

"It's right there. Paved in stone!"

"Hand it over!" Glennhard yelled as he tightened the grip around Vanessa's neck, the gun against her temple.

"First things first. I want her over here!"

"I'm not in a kidding mood, Heathrow!"

His eyes fell on his left pocket.

"Pull your left hand out of the pocket!"

He didn't so much as move.

"Heathrow!"

"Shove her over here and I'll give you the crystal. All you need to do is insert it into the hard drive and it will erase the whole program," he shouted back.

"Go and get the crystal!" he ordered the driver.

Under pressure, Mike handed it over without resistance. He watched as the man walked back with the code, toward Vanessa and her kidnaper.

"Now let her go, Glennhard!"

He smirked.

"You didn't think I would let you two live after this little ordeal? Now did you?"

He dragged the gun down, along Vanessa's neck, yet just as his index finger was about to brush the trigger, Mike shot once through his left pocket, hitting the driver's leg almost instantly. He fell onto the cold concrete floor with a scream.

On a whim, Glennhard took off with his *detainee* through the rear door by which he had entered the room. Mike began to run toward them in an attempt to follow, but just as he reached the door, the driver shot two bullets, one of which scraped Mike's knee. He stumbled forward and fell down the stairs.

When he had gotten back to his feet with unspeakable pain and trousers soaked with blood, Glennhard was already on the lot, running toward the pick-up truck while thrusting his hostage forward. She was screaming. But the screams were all Mike could hear as the truck dashed through the barbwire fence and the engine roared on with fury.

Had he been able to run, he would have sprung for his car, but the injury was too much to bare for Mike, who scarcely managed to enter his vehicle and turn the engine on.

As he turned the wheel on 10th Avenue and the motor hummed down the junction, Roland answered his call with fervor in his voice.

"Mike? Did you f–?"

"I need the new location!" he interrupted, short of breath, his wound hurting all the more.

"Mike, are you okay?"

"Quick! She's in danger!"

Without lingering, Roland managed to give him an exact location.

Tyres screeched as he drew near the deserted building site and stopped just short of the ditch.

He pulled himself out of the car with soaring pain, gazing in desperation as he strove to locate the white pick-up truck in which he had cleverly hidden Vanessa's cell.

He staggered along the ditch. Roland was still on the phone.

"I can't see the van!" he shouted as he peered across the site, panting for air.

"It should be only a few yards in front of you. I don't get it, you should see it by now!"

Mike walked unsteadily. The heat weighed on his shoulders like a plague. Sweat ran down his forehead and filled his eyes.

"I don't s–"

At the other end of the line, Roland's pupils reflected his screen.

"You're right over it Mike! You're right there!"

His gaze fell to the concrete. There, at his feet, Vanessa's cell phone lay scattered under the sun.

He kneeled down to pick up the pieces.

"Mike? Are you still with me?"

"They threw her cell out of the van," he said with distress in his voice.

Just as he spoke the words and his gaze wandered up toward the dire horizon of skyscrapers gleaming in the heat, his eyes uncovered something in the ditch. He heard a sound. A moan.

He looked closer.

"Vanessa?"

"Oh my God," Roland sighed from the other end of the line, as though he was there to witness the scene.

"Help me," she cried, "I'm really hurt."

Her voice was weak and frail, her face covered with blood and injuries.

"Vanessa!" he shouted as he glided down the bank, hurting his injured knee a bit more.

"I can't feel my legs. Hey threw me out of the car Mike. They threw me out of the car at full speed."

Her face turned into a cramped grimace.

"Don't worry," he sighed as he laid a hand on her wounded cheek. "We'll take care of you!"

"She gave him one last glance. One he would never forget, then shed a tear before her eyes closed out the heat and its blinding beams of light.

***

The patio looked onto the sea. Beneath it, palm trees were swaying in the wind. A warm breeze brushed against the silk curtains with grace as their shadows danced against the white wooden wall. Mike walked past the flowers on his left and took a seat in the sun. The air smelt of salt and aged wood. It shed a sense of calm and serenity.

He pulled out a cigarette from the left pocket of his shirt. He had never been much of a smoker, but turning into a health freak now would come across as outdated.

The waves drifted ashore in pleasant harmony. Mike watched as they caressed banks of white sand, wiping away footsteps after strollers and passer-bys. The sound they shed rocked like a cradle. He took a sip of his drink. It felt fresh and new, just like everything else. Perfect.

Against the warm wooden floor, bare feet brushed graciously towards him. They were that of a female.

She drew near him from behind and laid her hands on his shoulders. His eyes remained closed, longing to feel the warmth of the sun, longing to breathe in the way that it felt.

She grabbed a seat next to him and sighed in relief.

"It's a wonderful day," she said as her fingers ran through his hair.

"Everyday is a wonderful day," he replied and touched her hand with affection.

She looked at him, pondering. The wind stroked her raven hair.

"There's something I would like to ask you," she said, hesitantly. "You never told me–"

"Vanessa, don't!" he interrupted.

His eyes remained closed, sealed like a secret not ready to be uncovered.

A brief silence followed, aside from the sound of the sweet morning breeze brushing against the leaves and the foliage in the trees.

"I need to know," she insisted smoothly.

Mike opened his eyes. His gaze met with hers only to uncover glimmering pupils not quite dying from curiosity.

He sighed deeply as he thought of the right words to say.

"Did I...?" she intended to ask, yet paused in the middle.

Mike's gaze fell downwards.

Silence dawned again.

"We tried to reanimate you. We did the best we could."

She stared back at him with a thousand questions in her eyes.

He rose from his chair and walked toward the fence where he peered out at the sea and its never-ending horizon.

"Mike...?"

He stood with his back turned to her.

"Doctors said the injuries were too severe. They had to put you in an artificial coma." He paused. "That's the state you are in now." He paused again. "In the real world, that is."

She gazed at him almost relieved, as though contented that she didn't *really* die.

"There's one thing I don't understand," she asked.

"Yes?"

His eyes were still stuck on the beautiful horizon soaring before them.

"How come Glennhard didn't succeed in erasing the hard drive? He had the crystal code didn't he?"

Mike dug out the mysterious device from his pocket. The one he had been carrying all along, since the very beginning until the end of the *physical world* as they now referred to it. He held it in the palm of his hand.

"You see this? This is a portal between this world and the former one. Without it, the code is worthless. Everything goes through this device."

She smiled.

"What happened to Glennhard?"

"He ended up like the rest of them."

"What do you mean?"

"Only people with no criminal record were transferred here. In other words, the entire humanity, save for the unworthy. We couldn't afford them in a perfect world. They were left to die in the physical one. I believe they all died out by now. It's been years, has it not?"

"What if they reproduced and carried on the human race there?

"Not a chance. The only thing left *there*…" he said *there* with aversion in his voice, as though he was talking about a horrible place, eons from here, that no longer had the right to exist "…are animals and plants. And the generator of course. The others were all castrated and imprisoned until they faced final extinction."

She gave him a glance filled with apprehension.

He noticed and replied; "We couldn't have them in a perfect world. They had to go."

"I understand," she sighed.

The breeze cooled her down a bit as she leaned back in the shade cast by the parasol.

"What I don't understand is how you managed to get this thing through on time, before I… before I died."

Mike answered on a whim, not quite unwisely.

"You're not dead!" he retorted. You're in an artificial state of coma. And so am I by the way. We're the only ones whose physical bodies are still connected to the generator back there."

He grimaced again.

"But how did you manage to get the project through?"

"Before you d–" He stopped. "Before they sedated you, I was given one last moment with you."

Tears almost filled his eyes.

"Yes?"

"And there, I promised you that no matter what happens…" He hesitated. "No matter what! I gave you the promise that I will give you a new life, here in this brave new world. And that we will live forever, you and I, just like the other 10 billion people whose *minds* were also transferred."

"How did you get past the E.O.P.A? I mean how–"

"Jason Patterson," he uttered flatly before she even had the chance to finish her sentence.

She frowned, yet not in anger.

"You gave me his number. I told him we could save you. I told him we could–"

"Hush, don't speak."

She was close to him now. Standing behind by the fence, breathing against his neck, her forearm wrapped around his shoulder as if to say *I love you*. But the words never quite came out.

Instead, months passed by, each morning more beautiful than the last, the sea growing bluer everyday, it seemed, just like the sky which soared above it.

Months passed by and eventually they turned into years and then decades, the flavor of which exceeded all expectations. For there was no pain, no sorrow, no darkness nor shadows.

Until one day.

Until one odd and sad day when it all started, just like that, dawning on them out of the blue like a throng of clouds coming down from the skies.

Mike was the first who woke up to the sound of raindrops beating against the panes and that of the wind whistling through the blinds. He came to from a weary sleep, thinking it must be a nightmare. But the thought caught up with him, there were no nightmares in the perfect brave new world that he had created. He had seen to it that it couldn't happen.

Hastily, he leaped out of bed and sprang for the window. He stopped short of the glass and peered out at the horizon, squinting. The waves were relentless, collapsing upon one another with a fury only reminiscent of *the old world*.

"What the hell is that?" Mike mumbled as a thunderclap struck the sea in a livid yet beautiful lightning.

The wind seemed to blow harder now, shoving the water to an inescapable fate as it crashed against the shore in a crescendo of white, boiling foam.

This cannot be, he thought but didn't say.

"Mike, why are you not in bed? What's going on?" Vanessa asked wearily as she strove to open her eyes.

Michael didn't so much as turn around to give her a glance. Instead, he dashed for the phone, but before he even had the time to dial any virtual number, it rang with insatiable vigor.

"Mike! Mike?"

"Ronald what's–"

"Put on the news, mate! This is really worse than you think! It's all over the globe!"

Without lingering he turned on the TV which, ever since the very first day in the perpetually sunny virtual world, had not needed to abide to any weather forecasts. Up until now, breaking news reports had always been about good news or good things, save for that morning it seemed, as the silver screen depicted no other picture but that of dread and horror.

"They're talking about a storm. A major storm!" he said with stapled breath as he wiped his eyes.

"One never seen before," Ronald answered, not quite in dread.

"I don't understand! I can't grasp–"

"There's more to it, Mike. Much more to it," he said so flatly that it literally scared the hell out of him.

"What...?"

His voice quivered.

"They're after you, mate. They want explanations."

"What's going on?" Vanessa retorted as she witnessed her husband's pale visage and quavering lips.

Ronald carried on spitting painful words.

"What do you mean earthquakes, Ronald?"

"They're talking about a tsunami. It might hit the shore in eight hours or so. But we don't know yet..."

Speechless, Mike hung up, casting a sideways glance at his wife, one of those looks you only give when everything is–

"Everything's out of hand," he said flatly, mouth agape, almost unaffected now.

There was a scream, followed by the sound of breaking glass and that of shattered metal.

"It came from outside," Vanessa said as she tightened the belt of her dressing gown and crossed her arms above it as though they could shelter her.

Mike ran back to the window and gazed downwards. What his eyes encountered could not be explained in words. To his astonishment, what looked like a riot had developed down his street, giving way to a scene of sheer and total dismay, as if taken straight out of a horror movie.

Before his eyes, *they* were, plundering stealing, assaulting, stabbing and firing at will in a concussion of blood and pillage.

Children shrieked, women broke down in tears, tears that almost instantly filled his blood-red eyes.

He opened the door and walked out on the patio.

"Don't!" she yelled, but he was already out.

Gusts of wind slapped his face. He peered at the horizon, which used to be made of water, but as the sea retreated slowly before his eyes, he knew it would only be a matter of hours before land took its place, to eventually give way to that immense, highly dreaded tidal wave.

He fell to his knees, bowing his head in shame. Vanessa hurried out to embrace him. Lightning struck just a few yards from their patio as thunder roared in a blend of wrath and fury unleashed.

She dragged him inside and closed the glass door.

"Something went wrong in the old world. Something with the computer generator."

He dug out the mysterious device and held it in his trembling hands.

"I've gotta go back," he said, his voice quavering.

Vanessa kneeled down by his side.

"Let me come with you!"

"I wish it were possible, but you're..." He paused and sobbed.

"I'm what? Speak!"

"Your body in the physical world is way too injured to wake you up. And even if I could wake you up, it would only cause you tremendous physical pain."

She stared back at him, tears in her glimmering eyes.

"I'm the only one who can go back and fix this. I know I can fix this!"

"But—"

"There's no but! This is the only chance that we stand!" he bellowed as he began to dial numbers on the device, the silver screen of which seemed more grey and somber than ever.

***

Mike's eyelids opened to the sound of whistling birds and the hum of an otherworldly wind. Wearily, he sat up in bed – *or what served as a bed* – and unwired the cables from his body. It was not painful, yet unpleasant. He was wearing a white gown, the texture of which seemed as cold as the four walls surrounding him.

Above his head, a tiny window let faint beams of sunlight penetrate the computer generator room, embracing two giant hard drives, one of which seemed as dead as the rest of the planet – *save for the animal life that is –*.

He got up to his feet. His head was aching and his temples throbbing. Wearily, he strove as his eyes got accustomed to the frail light cast across the room. His muscles ached and his back felt frail.

He struggled towards the computer screen and turned the power switch on.

Without lingering, it lit up not quite like one of those thunderclaps in the brave new world. To his astonishment, the screen was blurred and shattered with interference.

Even though, he recognized the disfigured face of Rolnald. Beside him, Vanessa was staring at the screen in unspeakable unease.

"Do y- read me, M-?" Ronald shouted from behind the screen, his voice barely getting through the incessant noise.

"Ronald! I read you! I'm fine. I'm checking out the generator, one of the hard drives is completely dead!"

"This -s unb-rable Mi-e! Th- first -nami struck t-e shores of C-lif-rn-a. Half the -te is wi-d o-t!"

"Come again?"

"H-f -e sta-e is w-pe- out!"

"Hold on mate! I'm checking on the drive!"

"Hurry M-ke, this is unb-rabl-, unbear-le! We cannot st-d it anym-re!"

Mike kneeled down and did his best to uncover the hard drive failure, and before he laid eyes on the burned up, not to say carbonised, memory circuits, Ronald screamed all the more from behind the screen.

"Th- -s -ll!"

"What?"

"-is –s h-!"

"I don't read you Ronald! Come again!"

"Th-s i- hell!"

Mike glared back at the screen, holding the burned circuits in the palm of his trembling hands. His forehead ghastly with sweat, he didn't so much as speak when he heard the thunder strike behind their window and shattered glass filled their room almost instantaneously.

Although he could no longer see her face because of the noise on the screen, he heard Vanessa shriek. It was the most horrible shriek he had ever heard and as he heard Ronald's next words, he dropped the circuits which went crashing against the cold, bare floor.

"Ev-ryth-ng is worsen-ng for ev-ery min-te p--sed!"

And as Mike's gaze wondered to the screen of the second computer hard drive, revealing twice the amount of terabytes that it had initially, everything dawned on Mike with unspeakable horror.

The hard drive that had been used as a counterbalance to store and seal out all negative equations and events had crashed, causing all the stored information to get backed-up and transferred towards the other hard-drive, governing over all positive equations and thus the brave new world.

"We're b-rning out, M--e! The sun is c-m-ng on too strong! Th-re ar- fires now! M-ke Mi-e?"

The picture on the screen was gone now. Yet Mike glared at it with an empty gaze. The noise grew all but thinner and Ronald's voice began to fade away.

With tears in his eyes, he leaned over the microphone and said; " I cannot fix it!"

"Th-s -s hell! Pl-ase help -s! It's too h-t! Oh -y God. it's w-y too hot!"

"I cannot fix it!" Mike screamed at the top of his lungs! I cannot fix it!"

Once again, he heard Vanessa shriek out in pain amongst all the noise and interference. Yet he could no longer recognize her voice.

The only thing recognizable now were Ronald's words.

"W-'re burn--g out now! We'r- bur-ing out but we're n-t dy-ng!"

"What?

"W-'re not dyin-!"

"I can't fix it! I can't fix it!"

"M-ke y-u have g-t to help us! Th-s -s h-ll!"

"What?

His voice quavered.

"This his hell!"

Panic-stricken. he hit the keys randomly in an endeavor to crack the code, hoping for some kind of miracle and craving that God would see this and shed some light.

But tears blurred his vision and Vanessa's shrieks blurred his mind, the next words spoken by Ronald hit him like a thousand bricks.

"P-t an end to th-s endle-s s-ffering! Put an end t- this et-rnal h-ll! Turn o-f th- comp-ter!"

"Come again?" he pretended as if he didn't hear.

"Shut of- th- progr-m!"

"What?"

"Shut off the brave new world!"

IMMORTAL   *Erik Jayce Landberg*

ABOUT THE AUTHOR

*Erik Jayce Landberg is a Swedish author, short story
writer, artist and renowned musician.
He resides in the city often referred to as The Venice Of
Northern Europe, namely Stockholm.*

Erik Jayce Landberg

IMMORTAL   *Erik Jayce Landberg*

"Immortal" is taken from the Short Story Collection **"Fear Of The Dark"**
ISBN 978-1-105-64256-2 (Paperback)
ISBN 978-1-105-64928-8 (Dust Jacket Hard Cover)

Also available on Victoria Publishing Ltd.

www.ingramcontent.com/pod-product-compliance
Lightning Source LLC
Chambersburg PA
CBHW061456170626
46811CB00004B/1535